DEADLY PUZZLE

DAVID HUGHES

A Lazy Beagle Entertainment Publication

http://www.lazybeagleentertainment.com/

Deadly Puzzle

©Copyright Lazy Beagle Entertainment

Cover Art by Rondal Markwell

©Copyright by Lazy Beagle Entertainment

Edited by Theresa Ledford and Patrick Wendling-Markwell

This is a work of fiction. All characters, places and events are from the author's imagination and should not be confused with fact. Any resemblance to persons, living or dead, events or places is purely coincidental.

<u>WARNING: This book contains graphic violence and content which is only suitable for mature readers. This book also contains only scenes of homosexuality. There is NO sexual activity in this story.</u>

ONE

A wad of paper sailed through the air landing in the middle of the bonfire at Camp Seaward Bound. Charles, the head counselor glanced at it briefly before turning back to the group of teenagers surrounding him as he handed over an envelope and a trophy. He had just awarded Jennifer first prize for Best Short Story. The last few days it had been storming so badly, they had not had the opportunity to get out on the water and do any sailing.

Camp Seaward Bound is a camp for privileged teenagers who wanted to learn how to sail. In reality, it is just a place for parents to dump their kids for the summer while they go away on vacations or when they leave on long business trips.

Since the camp had been shut down for sailing because of the weather and they were on an isolated island, the camp counselors had decided to have each of the campers write a short story and as a reward for the best short story, that camper would get to come back the next summer for free and receive a free family pack of tickets for a cruise.

Jennifer had won the contest and just as she accepted the trophy, grinning from ear to ear, the fire exploded causing people to jump and scream. Fireworks were popping and flaring up causing everyone to scatter. Therefore no one noticed when an arm slipped around Jennifer holding a knife and slit her throat. Blood spurted and she dropped the trophy on the ground, clutching at the gaping gash across her throat. She stumbled around for a moment before finally collapsing onto the ground her hair landing in the flames catching fire. The fire quickly burned her hair and spread to her scalp before dirt was kicked on it.

When the campers and counselors finally calmed down enough to come back to the fireside, pandemonium ensued when they found the dead body of their fellow camper. Charles reached into his pocket for his phone to call the mainland authorities and came up empty. He looked around wildly and found the counselors were all huddling together with the campers and directed them back to the cabins. As they hurried off he told them to get the campers settled into the mess hall and then to meet him in his office.

Ten minutes later after tearing his office apart he realized there was not going to be any help coming. His cell phone was missing, his computer had been destroyed, the land line phone on his desk had been smashed and the lines cut. The phone jacks in the wall had been cemented up as well. He left his office and headed down the hall to the camp medical office and heard more screams.

He turned and looked around wildly for the location of the screams and heard another one; they were coming from the mess hall. Sprinting he darted into the door and saw all the campers and counselors gathered around the table at the front where he and the other counselors ate their meals while they watched over their charges. The counselors pulled the campers out of the way to let him through.

There on the table in front of him was a box. A crudely written message on the top proclaimed:

TO SOLVE THIS MYSTERY YOU MUST ASSEMBLE THE PUZZLE LOCATED WITHIN. SOME PIECES NOT INCLUDED.

Charles reached out a shaking hand and opened the box. Inside was a makeshift puzzle made out of cork board. Each piece had part of a picture glued to it. He grabbed a few pieces and saw that each piece had the face of either a camper or a counselor on it.

Turning he said, "All of you get to the tables right now and try to be quiet. Rick and Matthew, please stand guard at the front door. Carl, you and Katrina go to the back kitchen door. Lisa, you and Jesse help me assemble this puzzle quickly."

The counselors scattered and those not named herded the campers to the tables. The air was tense and Charles was starting to sweat with frayed nerves.

His hands trembled as he picked out the edges of the puzzle. Looking into the box he saw something at the bottom of the box and reached in to grab it. It was a group photo of the campers and counselors, himself included. A red drop of blood was blotting out the face of Jennifer. He set the photo down on the tabletop as Lisa and Jesse started assembling the puzzle.

After ten minutes the puzzle was completed, even with the drop of blood on the piece that had the face of Jennifer.

Lisa looked up at him and said, "Charles the puzzle piece with Jesse's face is not here." She glanced over at Jesse and saw the color drain out of his face.

Jesse plunged his hand into his pockets

and said, "I am calling the police!" He yanked his right hand out of his pants pocket exclaiming in pain. Stuck to the palm was a small needle. He pulled the needle out of his palm and dropped it on the ground. "My phone is missing!"

Charles said, "Mine is too and my computer and land-line are also destroyed." All over the mess hall people started searching their pockets for their phones. Charles did not need to hear anything from them because he knew what the result would be; all of their phones would be missing.

"Ch-Ch-Charles…"

Charles turned to look at Jesse. In his hand was a puzzle piece. "This was in my left pants pocket.

Charles reached out and took the piece from him and put it into the puzzle on the tabletop. They glanced down at it and back up at each other. Lisa backed away from Jesse as if he were carrying the plague.

Jesse started shaking and convulsing,

frothing at the mouth. Within ten seconds he had collapsed onto the ground falling still, eyes glazed and terrified staring into nothing as the life left his body.

"The campers began to scream and panic erupted in the hall. Everyone made a mad dash for the doors, trampling each other. Charles tried to get everyone to calm down, but within moments everyone had fled out of the hall except for Lisa and the other counselors. They all gathered around him staring down at the dead body of Jesse.

Lisa grabbed a napkin off the nearest table and bent to retrieve the needle off the ground where Jesse had dropped it. "I bet you anything this thing was covered in some type of poison. It is the only thing that can explain what happened to him."

Charles nodded in agreement. "Okay everyone. We have someone out there killing off counselors and campers."

Everyone began to look around at each

other in suspicion.

"Well, one way or another, we need to figure this thing out. Each of you go out in pairs, Lisa with me, and round up those kids. Do not let them out of your sight! Bring them back here to the mess hall and lock them inside. No camper is to be left without supervision. Got that?" Charles looked around and everyone acknowledged him. "Good, let's go."

They all ran out of the hall and headed off in various directions to start rounding up the campers. Charles looked down at Lisa and saw that, though terrified, she was also very determined. She smiled grimly at him and they started walking off to look for the campers.

"We will get out of this Lisa, I promise," stated Charles emphatically. He looked down to smile at her and she was no longer there. Turning to look behind him, he saw her hanging from a noose in the tree. Sticking out of her mouth was the edge of another puzzle piece. The picture of her face in the completed puzzle back in the mess hall was devoid of blood. This piece had a drop of blood on it.

Charles turned to look around him more frightened than before. He had a bad feeling about all of this.

TWO

The only thing Charles could think to do was go and cut her down, but then remembered when the police eventually showed up, they would not be happy to have him tampering with the crime scene. He turned back around and started out cautiously looking around simultaneously for any of the campers or another one of the counselors. Over near the remains of the bonfire where Jennifer had died he saw the fire poker lying on the ground.

He ran over to retrieve it and briefly considered grabbing the knife off the ground but remembered it was evidence in a crime. He started to walk away then decided he did not care and raced back to grab it off the ground realizing he could use it for self-defense and he certainly did not want it being used against him or another counselor, much less one of the campers.

Thrusting the knife through his belt he

peered around him warily and ran to the nearest tree, scaled it as quickly as he dared and took a look around him. He saw three campers and a counselor not too far off and then almost fell out of the tree when an arrow transfixed one of the campers in the face. Screaming, the counselors grabbed the two remaining campers left alive and started running.

Scrambling out of the tree he started yelling at them to turn around and run the other way since they were running toward the beach instead of the mess hall. He tried to overtake them but a shot rang out and he watched in horror as one of the counselors stumbled and fell, half of her head missing. The campers and remaining counselor lost all sense of sanity and fled, running in complete opposite directions from one another.

Charles raced for the camper closest to him and caught him by the arm. He let out a shriek and struggled to break free, bashing Charles on the hand with a rock, but he determinedly held on and yanked the kid to him, sheltering his body with his. Bodily picking him up, he ran as fast as he could back to the mess hall.

The camper finally stopped struggling and fainted in his arms. Once inside the mess hall he saw six campers and two counselors inside huddled against the far wall, all holding knives for protection. One of the female campers screamed and threw her knife, but as she didn't know what she was doing, cut herself instead as the knife tumbled to the ground about two feet away from her. Charles quickly deposited the unconscious camper with the group and ripped his shirt off. He tore a strip off the bottom and wrapped her hand up as tight as he dared.

Looking up he saw that one of the adults there was not actually a counselor, but was instead the camp doctor. Instead of treating the camper he was staring straight ahead with his mouth open. Stapled to his forehead was a puzzle piece with a drop of blood.

"How the hell did you guys not see that Michael is dead," shouted Charles.

Startled, everyone turned to look then scrambled away from the body hurriedly. The part of his shirt around his stomach was tented out. Gently Charles reached out and lifted the hem of his shirt and they all saw a small hatchet protruding from the doctors stomach. His last act of bravery after having been hit in the stomach had been to herd these six campers to safety. Apparently after being hit in the stomach with the hatchet at close range the killer had also stapled a puzzle piece to his head.

Charles ripped it off his forehead and started to fling it savagely aside when the door opened and something was tossed inside the mess hall. The girl he had bandaged screamed again, this time fainting.

Charles stood up quickly and ran to retrieve the item which turned out to be a little sandwich baggie with four puzzle pieces in it. Examining them he noticed the piece for the camper who had been shot with the gun the counselor for the arrow and two others, one counselor and the chef for the camp. He stood up and walked to the puzzle up on the table and stared down at it.

He noticed that another piece had been replaced while they were all gone. The youngest camper, a young man named Jason, now had a drop of blood on his face. The piece with his face unmarked was inside the puzzle box. Pulling the piece for Lisa out of his pocket and adding it to the four from the baggie and the one for the doctor, he plucked the pieces out of the puzzle and added the bloody pieces to the puzzle. As a whole, the puzzle was looking like a bad walking nightmare, slowly coming to life.

Staring down at the grisly scene before him he felt tears sliding down his face and watched as one slid to the tip of his nose, wavered momentarily, and fell to the puzzle, mixing with the droplet of blood on Jason's face. He swiped his hand across his eyes, took a deep breath and whirled around to look at the people in the hall with him. They were all staring at him expectantly, and he noticed they had all shifted their positions to get away from the dead doctor lying on his side, vacant eyes staring at the door.

Opening his mouth to speak some type of encouraging words he was interrupted by a scream of terror. Bolting to the door he barked out, "Stay here with these kids!' Flinging open the door he stared in horror at the sight ahead of him. Hanging upside down by a chain from a pole that had been erected in the middle of the bonfire was one of the female campers. She was screaming as the flames from the bonfire engulfed her. Racing toward her he knew there was nothing he could do, but he felt he had no other choice.

Halfway to the bonfire a figure stepped out of the shadows with a machete in his hand. Charles skidded to a stop and stared saying, "You?" before the blade connected with his throat severing his head from his body.

The killer stuck two puzzle pieces to the blade using the blood as a sort of glue, dropped the sword onto the body of the dead head counselor then turned and melted back into the shadows.

THREE

Water crashed onto the beach as over in a small outcrop of rocks two figures struggled. Finally, one of the figures reached up and struck the other in the head with a rock, knocking him semi-unconscious. When the male camper stopped struggling and slumped forward a little, the killer grabbed the back of his head and shoved it face first into the waters of a tide pool and held his face under. The boy regained consciousness, but was not strong enough or capable enough at the moment to fight back and soon lost the fight, drowning.

When the camper beneath him finally died the killer stood up, pulled a small box out of his jacket pocket and opened it. He had to pull a mini flashlight out as well and turn it on to see what he was doing. Shuffling through the pieces he finally found the right one and dropped it onto the camper's outstretched body, turned around and walked back toward the mess hall.

Crouching down on the ground beside the wall, hiding in the shadows he waited.

He did not have long to wait. Two minutes later he saw a counselor and two campers running hurriedly toward the mess hall. He stepped out of the shadows and yelled out, "Oh thank god! I have been hiding here forever waiting for someone. There is a dead body down there by the water."

The counselor paused in running and waited until the campers disappeared inside the doors to the mess hall and then hurried over to him not knowing what danger he was in. The killer reached out, grabbed the counselor when he got close enough to him and snapped his neck dropping another puzzle piece on his body then hurried off to the front of the mess hall. He opened the door quietly and peered inside. Eight campers and three counselors were standing up at the table examining the puzzle.

He stepped inside and slammed the door,

putting his back against it. The campers and counselors whirled around, one of the girls putting a hand up to her mouth to cover a scream. He almost laughed spoiling everything.

"Where is everyone," he asked?

One of the counselors looked at him and said, "Charles is dead and so are several other counselors and campers. Everyone else is still out there somewhere. Did you see anything out there?"

He nodded and said, "There is a dead counselor outside at the back of the mess hall with his neck snapped and a male camper, I think it is Ronnie with his head under water in one of the tide pools down at the beach in that rocky outcropping." I was trying to hide down by the water and was looking for a boat, but they are all capsized. I saw someone running and ran after him and watched him lure a counselor away from two campers that were coming in here and then he broke his neck and ran toward the trees up past the bonfire. Before he ran off I watched him drop something on top of the counselor. I ran in here as fast as I could."

One of the counselors cursed under his breath and he and one other counselor ran outside. Five minutes later they were back and they had two puzzle pieces. Sighing one of the counselors replaced two puzzle pieces with what they had in their hands.

"That leaves nineteen campers and four counselors unaccounted for still alive; unless the killer got to some we have not yet discovered. I don't like to say it, but we can't help them. We all need to stay in here and wait for help to arrive. Counting us here, there are twenty-eight campers and seven counselors remaining, though we only know that we are alive. The others may be dead or alive and none of us know." He put his face in his hand briefly then sat down.

Before anyone could stop her, one of the female counselors reached out, grabbed a knife and plunged it into her stomach three times before finally collapsing onto the ground blood pooling around her. Everyone hastily jumped back to avoid the blood and one of the female campers screamed, her eyes rolled into the back of her head, and she passed out.

Three campers and one of the counselors, along with the killer, ran outside screaming and dispersed in different directions.

FOUR

Carol opened her eyes and looked around. The last thing she remembered was someone sneaking up behind her and then nothing. She tried to reach up behind her head to feel the lump on the back of her head, but her hands were tied to something. Forcing her eyes open further she looked around.

That was when she realized one of the male counselors was tied up beside her and they were in one of the counselor's golf carts that they used to get around the island on. Her hands were tied to the steering wheel. When she tried to say something she realized she couldn't and saw with horror that the counselor's lips had been sewn shut and saw in the little rear view mirror that hers were as well.

Hearing a soft laugh behind her she turned her head as far as it would go and saw a figure in the shadows behind the golf cart holding something in his hand. Noticing for the first time that the golf cart was actually running and her foot was pushed down on the pedal. She tried to move her foot off the pedal but the sharp pain in her foot forced her to stop and she tried to scream in pain but the threads sewing her mouth shut almost ripped out causing even more pain.

Tears streaming down her face she turned and looked behind her again. Finally with a cry of shock, her lips ripped open causing her to gasp as her lips were shredded and blood flooded her mouth. She recognized the killer and started to say something when he raised the object he had been holding; it was a bloody hatchet. He swung it down and chopped a rope holding the golf cart in place and she watched as he dropped two small puzzle pieces to the ground behind the golf cart as it launched forward and hurtled over the cliffs edge.

FIVE

James was jogging slowly around the island keeping a wary eye out as he held a knife in one hand, looking around as he went without breaking stride. He was the top cross country and track star at his high school back in NYC where he lived so he knew he could keep this up if he took it slowly. He figured this was better than waiting around out there on the island or in one of the cabins. Some psycho was out there killing off his fellow campers and the counselors and he had no intention on being one of the dead bodies.

Hearing a noise he stopped jogging momentarily and looked around. Seeing a seagull attack a crab he smiled and started jogging again. He was just nervous and every little noise was a killer in his mind's eye.

***

Carey had run all the way to the

boathouse to get her boat and get off the island as quickly as she could but when she got there she saw her boat had been chopped up so she just sat down on the floor and had been crying ever since. She knew she was making a lot of noise but she was too scared to stop crying.

She heard the sound of running footsteps outside and covered her mouth to stifle the sound of her sobbing. She shrank back into the shadows as the door to the boathouse opened and she could make out the outline of someone standing there looking around. Finally she recognized him and scrambled out of the cover of her hiding place and ran over to him throwing her arms around him. He put his arms around her and hugged her before he drove a screwdriver through her eye and dropped her onto the floor laughing softly shoving the other puzzle piece into her one remaining eye.

He turned and sauntered out of the boathouse closing the door behind him before ramming the screwdriver into the soft wood of the door with Carey's eye still impaled on it.

SIX

Three girls were hiding in the closet of their cabin waiting for the police to arrive and rescue them. Clarissa and Shya had fallen asleep next to Rachelle and she was starting to doze off herself when the closet door opened suddenly. She gasped then sighed in relief as she recognized the guy standing in front of her. She reached out and shook Clarissa and Shya awake. When they saw who was standing there, they all stood up and started to walk out of the closet.

As they walked out of the closet they were all impaled on a long sharpened broom handle as he shoved it into Clarissa's belly and through Rachelle and Shya behind her.

"Fucking twittery bitches. I hate snobby little socialite whores like you." He grunted and gave the broomstick handle an extra twist eliciting a gasp of pain from the girls, then shoved them back into the closet. He watched as they bled out and died before closing the door on them dropping three puzzle pieces onto the ground.

***

James had just finished another circle around the island when he stepped into a small hole twisting his ankle. He grunted in pain and yanked his foot out. After examining his ankle he realized he could jog no further. He had to find a place to hide and quickly. Turning around he looked around and saw a small copse of trees a little ways in from the beach and made his way over to them.

As he got there he saw a figure step out of the shadows of the trees that kicked his legs out from under him. He landed hard on his back and as he was gasping for breath, trying to clear the stars from his vision he watched as a boot came hurtling toward his face.

He tried to roll out of the way quickly but he wasn't quick enough. The boot came down hard on his face again and again. Within moments he was being kicked all over and he could feel bones breaking all over and he began to lose consciousness. His last thought before he died was that he would never get to compete in his senior year and celebrate his victories with Emily in her bedroom back at her house.

SEVEN

Kristin had been hiding in a sand dune for the last half hour and was petrified she was going to be killed any minute. On occasion she could hear distant conversations carried to her on the wind and echoes bouncing around the dunes. She knew her fellow campers and the counselors were being murdered. She had heard screaming and once a gunshot.

Suddenly there was the sound of a snapping twig and she finally bolted to her feet and almost collapsed; her right leg was asleep. Hearing the splashing of the waves crashing against the beach she headed for the water. About a quarter mile out from the very beach she was standing on was another small island, only about a quarter as large as this one, but it had a warren of caves she could hide in. She was the girls swim team captain and she knew she could make the distance easily.

She stretched her leg experimentally and stamped it down hard a couple of times to try and get it to wake up. When she felt she couldn't wait around any longer she hunched low, looked around her and set off for the water's edge. Before she entered the water she glanced around one last time and seeing no one, she plunged into the water bracing herself for the chill of the Atlantic. She did a few quick warm-up exercises knowing if she didn't she might cramp up in the water, though she did them hurriedly because she was in full view of anyone who might look down and see her.

Kristin plunged headfirst into the water and started swimming in the direction of the little island. After a minute of swimming underwater she surfaced and began doing a powerful breaststroke then lapsed into a front crawl while using a flutter kick with her feet to propel her body faster through the water.

After another two minutes she began to tire. Normally a swim like this would take her about four and a half minutes, but this was open water in the middle of the Atlantic and the water was very choppy. A minute later she stopped swimming and simply floated in the water on her back allowing her body to go limp, on occasion fluttering her feet in the water to keep her afloat. If she started to drift away from the general direction in which she was headed, she would use her arms to start heading in the proper direction again.

Even in these conditions she would have made it by now, but the adrenaline had been pumping through her body ever since those fireworks had gone off and they discovered the body of Jennifer with her throat slit. She had never particularly liked Jennifer, but she hadn't disliked her either. Jennifer was one of those girls who was popular because she was pretty but she never let that go to her head because she was also the head of the Science Club, tried out for every student play and musical, was the Vice President of the Student Council and was taking all AP classes. She never bullied anyone and she included everyone in her activities no matter who they were. It was hard to like her yet also hard to dislike her. Too perky yet in this day and age one could never be sure of the motives of a person like that.

She shuddered just thinking about Jennifer and decided to get going again. She rolled over onto her stomach and resumed swimming. After two minutes she saw the island ahead of her and started swimming more vigorously. Finally Kristin had to stand and splash ashore. Without stopping to breathe she headed straight for the cave system. They had all explored these before and knew they were empty so she plunged directly into one without a second thought longing for some peace until they could all be rescued.

She stopped just inside one when she saw a tiny light. There on the ground in front of her was a small wooden box and through a small hole was a beam of light. Hesitating only a moment she bent down and ripped the top off seeing a small lit lantern. Moments later the hissing head of a cobra reared its head out of the box and before she could move away, struck forward repeatedly sinking its fangs into her face.

EIGHT

Dolores, Marie, Nancy, Kay and Kathy were all sitting in a tree in the woods shaking with fear. The noise of something hard hitting the base of the tree caused Dolores to scream. Looking down after covering her mouth she saw the body of Kristin laying there, dead with a puzzle piece glued to her head. Kathy bit back a moan of terror and clambered down from the tree, took one look at Kristin and began to run.

A figure stepped out of the bushes and brought a rock down on her head, crushing the skull killing her instantly. Holding up his hand the killer dropped the rock, reached into his pocket and searched through the little bag holding the puzzle pieces. After finding the right one, he dropped it on top of Kathy, looked up into the tree and said, "I see you pathetic little bitches up there. I am giving you a thirty second head start before I come after you."

Dolores, Marie, Nancy and Kay all jumped out of the tree and raced away, Dolores and Marie going together in one direction and Nancy and Kay in the other. After giving them the allotted thirty seconds he went after Dolores and Marie first.

Casually strolling out of the clearing he stumbled over a foot partially hidden in a bush and peered inside seeing the face of Mike staring back out at him. Reaching into the bushes he grabbed him by the hair and dragged him out before ramming a small branch into his throat dropping him to the ground where he finally stopped struggling, much less living. Finding and dropping the right puzzle piece on top of his lifeless body, he cursed his luck that he now had to search longer for Dolores and Marie. Dolores and Marie were twins as Nancy and Kay were twins, both sets identical.

Picking up his pace, the killer ran on tracking down the noisy twins Dolores and Marie. He hated them most of all out of everyone on the island and Nancy and Kay followed a close second. Eventually their haphazard struggling path through the forest lead him to the other side of the boat house. He walked around it looking in every possible hiding place before he finally found them hiding under a plastic tarpaulin.

They both screamed as he dragged them out, but he quickly stuffed their mouths and bashed them both in the head hard enough to stun them and silence them, but not enough to kill them or knock them out completely. Dragging their bodies out into the open where he had a little light he finally stood there staring down at them with loathing on his face.

Searching his pockets he finally found what he was looking for and pulled it out. It was a glove on which he had glued long razor sharp blades, each about an inch long, in the shape of thin fingernails; all painted a bright crimson red. Years before the twins had cornered him and thought it would be funny to poke him and claw at him with their fingernails and Dolores had accidentally punctured his upper lip with one of her fingernails and now he had a half moon shaped scar there above his top lip.

As he put the glove on he bent down over them and examined them. They were both about four feet nine inches tall with long dark brown hair that was straight and hung to the middle of their backs. They were ugly little bitches and worth more trouble to him alive than they were dead so he didn't take more time with them than he had to. He reached out and stabbed one of the nails through Dolores and Marie's upper lips, feeling the nail go through the maxilla as well.

The muffled screams made him laugh softly. He started jabbing the gloves down into their bodies at random spots giggling as they squirmed and fought their bonds. A moment later he heard someone coming towards them so he quickly dropped their puzzle pieces on top of them before driving the glove straight down through their throats leaving it behind and moved down onto the beach and hid behind a rock watching as two counselors found the bodies of Dolores and Marie.

NINE

Back in the Mess Hall the bloody puzzle sat on the table where it had been left. He had not been able to locate Nancy or Kay yet, but had found someone else.

Eva, the sagging potbellied camp counselor who taught the campers how to clean boats properly, had snuck into the mess hall thinking it was safest to hide in there where there were more likely to be more people.

However, when she entered the hall she found it to be completely empty. She rushed up to the top table and looked down at the puzzle. She found more puzzle pieces had been replaced with the ones covered with drops of blood. She backed up slowly and stopped, turning in her tracks as she heard a creaking noise. Seeing no one there Eva took a hesitant step forward and heard the creaking noise again; this time she noticed the noise was distinctly above her.

Slowly she looked above her afraid she might see a body dangling there, but instead she saw a large solid object. Eva stared at it mystified for a moment trying to figure out what exactly it was because it certainly didn't belong there. She should know, she spent more time in that hall than anyone gorging her puffy face while sneaking sips of various alcohols she could sneak past the boss. This was where she also came when she managed to talk someone into actually fucking her, which she usually had to pay for. She was on her back on this floor and these tables enough to know beyond any shadow of a doubt that it did not belong there.

She took a step forward and looked down at the same time and bumped into someone. Eva opened her mouth to scream when a hand covered it suddenly yanking her body forward and then throwing it to the ground. The hand still covered her mouth but she was able to see who it was and tried screaming harder. He pushed down on her head against the hard wood of the floor making sparkles of light burst in her vision. Finally it became too much and she stopped struggling.

Leaning over her he smiled, then reached into her mouth with a pair of industrial grade tongs, gripped her tongue tightly and waited for realization to take form in her eyes. She started to inhale and scream again but he ripped up and out with the tongs suddenly bringing her tongue with him and at the same time, turned and brought a knife swiftly across her stomach, effectively eviscerating her.

As Eva lay there dying he stared into her eyes and said, "Don't ever call me a faggot again witch. Oh wait," he smiled holding up her tongue, "you can't."

He took a puzzle piece out of his pocket and stuck it to her tongue which he then threw on the floor near the door. Bending down he yanked off her shoes and had to hold his nose at the stench emanating from her feet. Throwing them across the room he walked over to a table nearby and picked up a small shoe box. Pulling out the pair of high heels inside he held them up for her to see and said, "See, I will even give you the ruby slippers and striped stockings." These he pulled out of the box and held up alongside the shoes. The shoes were black but covered in red glitter so they sparkled in the light.

He walked back over to her and yanked the stockings up her legs then shoved the too small shoes onto her feet, breaking several toes in the process. He then walked backwards and wrapped around a nail in the wall he grabbed a rope and yanked on it. The hanging object crashed to the floor on top of Eva, crushing her body beneath it, but leaving her legs from the knees down uncovered. The object was a crudely built small house he had constructed of scrap wood, trash and stones from around the island.

"Now, a house has finally been dropped on the Wicked Witch. With any luck, Dorothy will come get your slippers and skip right into my blade." Laughing softly to himself he slipped around the pool of blood starting to pool out from beneath the trashed house, he quickly strode out of the Mess Hall through the door in the back of the kitchen and went hunting again.

TEN

Nancy tripped over a rock buried in the sand, arms flailing and grabbed for her sister Kay. Kay yanked hard on her arm and they managed to keep upright and started running full out again. Finally they came to a stop, Kay clutching her side where a stitch had developed, gasping for breath. Nancy looked around wildly for cover and finally spotted a large pile of boxes.

Pointing at them she and Kay hurried over to them making sure to look all around as they scurried for cover. From the print on the boxes, Nancy was able to determine they had once held supplies for repairing yachts. Some of them were rather large; in fact large enough to hold two teenage girls. She motioned to Kay and the two got into the boxes and pulled the lids closed, holding their breaths.

A few moments later the boxes started moving and a heavy weight settled on top of them. They screamed, even knowing how useless it would be at that point.

The killer was busy taping up both boxes. When he was done he placed two very large and heavy pieces of boat siding on the top of them and covered the siding with heavy rocks liberally saturating every square inch with gasoline, lit a match and flung it as he backed hurriedly away. Watching the flames roar into life he laughed when the twins started screaming. Backing up even further, he dropped two bloody puzzle pieces onto the ground and vanished into the slowly receding darkness.

ELEVEN

Michael cautiously stuck his head out from underneath the disabled Jeep he had been hiding successfully under ever since the murders started. Glancing around he swiftly pulled it back under and closed his eyes. He was hoping if he stayed quiet long enough the killer would think he had killed everyone and leave the island somehow or that he could at least get out from this hiding place and arm himself.

As Michael was busy plotting escape the killer was sitting on the ground not ten feet away from the Jeep watching his next victim breathing heavily. He had known he was here the whole time and had known he would not be leaving the spot until he was sure he was safe, though since it was a Jeep that sat fairly high off the ground and was in one of the better lit areas of the island it was an ignorantly stupid place to hide. Michael though was not known for his intelligence, but for his hideous idiocy, not to mention he also thought and acted like he was some black gangster. Instead he was only a severely overweight, whiny white guy with sexuality issues.

Realizing he could not afford the luxury of sitting around to wait for Michael to come out of hiding anymore he stood up and silently walked around the back of the Jeep, reached under softly and very quietly looped a noose around Michael's feet. He never felt it coming. The killer walked over to the other Jeep parked ten feet behind it, started the engine and jumped out rushing around to the front of the vehicle and activated the winch attached to the front end which hauled Michael kicking and screaming from under the Jeep.

Gripping the end of a heavy branch he struck Michael on the side of his head rendering him partially unconscious. Slipping back into the Jeep he turned off the engine and then slipped under the hood and disabled the engine.

As he finally found himself standing over the prone body of Michael he stared at him dispassionately before finally spitting on him. He took a small stapler out of his pocket and stapled a bloody puzzle piece to his forehead as he lay there staring up with glazed eyes.

He opened his mouth to plead then saw who it was standing above him. Gasping he struggled even harder to get away which forced the killer to smash him over the head again with the stout branch.

Quickly, he bent over Michael's prone form and sliced away all of his clothing, leaving the shredded fabric in a neat pile beside him, then grabbed him by his right arm and rolled him onto his stomach. Grabbing what looked to be a police baton from his belt he held it up admiring his handiwork.

Even though Michael could not respond, he was still conscious, just barely, and could hear him. "I got this idea from a certain vampire movie. Instead of a sword though, I fashioned blades at the end of the baton and have attached a small timer. When I turn the timer on, you will have thirty seconds before it rips your insides to shreds and lets you bleed to death, which can come slowly or quickly, I have no idea and I was hoping to have the time to watch but I have only a few people left around here to torture and kill. I was hoping you could be my last, but I have reserved that for one person and you really are in the end, just useless anyway." Quickly, and dry, he rammed the baton up Michael's ass and depressed the timer switch. "You have thirty seconds left Michael. I suggest you use those thirty seconds to enjoy the feeling."

Walking away he giggled a little under his breath. Just a few seconds later he heard an earsplitting scream and said, "So I lied; you only had twenty seconds." Pausing he thought a moment then turned back and walked over to where Michael lay sobbing and bleeding out on the ground. "You never should have raped me all those years ago. You deserve to suffer, but I can't take the chance someone will come along and find you, undoing all my efforts at planning out the perfect demise for you." He smiled evilly down at Michael as he turned his head and stared up at his killer. Pulling a knife out of his waistband, he plunged it down into the face staring up at him and walked away.

TWELVE

Andrew watched from hiding as Michael was slaughtered in the most horrific way imaginable. If the killer could do this to his own brother, he would certainly be able to tear him to pieces after what he had done to him. He turned to run off in the other direction and immediately fell to the ground. Glancing down in horror he saw his foot had been caught in a rope trap and tried to scramble free. Terror started to build in him as he heard the Jeep starting up and the engine revving.

The killer looked out at Andrew as he tried desperately to get away and started the winch up again dragging him towards the Jeep. Walking slowly he got into the Jeep, started the engine once again and revved it in order to strike more terror into his heart. It worked as Andrew struggled even harder though it was extremely difficult as he was being pulled along the ground.

Releasing the parking break and putting it into drive, he stomped on the gas pedal and raced forward screaming, "I am not your fucking hood ornament you piece of shit!" Two seconds later he ran over Andrew. Braking suddenly he threw it into reverse and backed over him. Over the next minute he ran over him repeatedly, then got out of the Jeep and wedged a heavy branch against the gas pedal and the bottom of the driver's seat. He reached in and released the parking brake and watched as the Jeep roared off dragging a lifeless Andrew with him into the ocean. He quickly dropped two puzzle pieces onto the ground next to Michael's prone body and vanished into the night.

THIRTEEN

Crystal slowed from a fast run to a very slow walk then realized she couldn't walk anymore at all. She was cramping something awful and standing there she glanced around for a place to hide. The only feasible place she could see to hide was a cabin about a hundred feet away to her left. Slowly, and with agonizing pain, she started walking toward it and climbed up onto the small porch. Grasping the door handle she twisted it and heard a strange click then rapid beeping. Horrified she tried to turn and run.

Watching from a safe distance the killer watched as Crystal turned seconds before the cabin exploded and followed the trail her head made as it sailed away from the force of the explosion and landed on the ground at his feet. He stomped on it over and over again before finally dropping a puzzle piece on top of the decimated head and vanished once again into the darkness.

FOURTEEN

Mike was hiding in a tree watching various macabre horror shows playing out around him. He couldn't help but notice the length of the grass under the tree he was hiding in and thought how it needed to be mowed. Too bad he would probably die before he got a chance to tend to it. As the groundskeeper he was responsible for the area in and around the camp to make sure it was all groomed and respectable looking. He sighed, took one last look around then pulled out a joint and a porn rag. If he was going to die, he might as well go out enjoying himself.

"You know, you never directly did anything to me, but you allowed it to happen and did nothing to intervene. You really think I am going to let you enjoy looking at that or getting high before I put a bullet in your head?"

Mike glanced down and shrugged his shoulders. "You ain't nothing to me, so it wasn't my fault." He turned back to his magazine and started to open it as he dragged a lighter out of his pocket.

"The only reason I am being quick with you is because I don't really give a shit about you. I have already killed Dolores so she won't be around to be your little bitch for you anymore anyway." He pointed the gun up into the tree, pulled the trigger and watched as Mike's lifeless body fell to the ground. He grabbed the joint and shoved it up Mike's nose then forced the porn magazine down his throat, dropped a puzzle piece on top of him and walked away aiming the gun at fellow camper Dave as he jumped out of the bushes near him and raced off. Pulling the trigger he watched as he kept running for a moment then toppled over face first, draw a shuddering breath and go still. Walking over he put a bullet in the back of his head to make sure he stayed down and dropped another puzzle piece on top of his head and walked off.

FIFTEEN

Slowly circling around a small storage shed, the killer listened carefully and determined the person hiding inside was none other than Jan. A thief and liar of the worst caliber always stealing from charities and making promises she refused to keep, all under the guise of helping. Anyone who knew her also knew her to be a conniving and manipulative bitch. Why she worked at the camp, no one knew, but there she was and she had pushed the killers buttons one too many times for him to allow her to live.

He kicked the door in and jumped sideways at the same time. Moments after he did a pitchfork came flying out of the open doorway followed by Jan. She started to scream but the killer whirled a machete in his hands and sliced right through her face. Before she could topple he yanked the blade back and thrust it into her protruding gut and watched her hit the ground.

Throwing down a puzzle piece he turned and melted into the shadows.

SIXTEEN

By the killers count, there were only fifteen campers and two counselors left, not counting himself. Directly in front of him was one of those counselors who thought she was protecting him from some "maniac" as she kept saying. Her name was Marcy. A few years ago she had slapped him and told him he was worthless as a human being simply because he didn't agree with her over the proper way to sign using American Sign Language. She herself was partially deaf as well as partially mute. He had grown up with an aunt and uncle who were both complete deaf mutes so was extremely conversant in using ASL as was Marcy.

No one ever called him worthless and got away with it. He tapped her on the shoulder to get her attention and she whirled around. He held up his hands and signed, "Are you ready?"

"Ready for what," she signed back?

"To die? You think I am worthless." He watched the burgeoning horror dawning in her eyes as she finally realized who the killer was. Before she could move, he quickly plunged a syringe into her neck and watched as her body became paralyzed and she sank to the ground crying in utter defeat.

He signed, "You know, all I had said back then was your interpretation of the phrase 'I love you' was different than the way I used it. I simply used a single sign and you used the words; same thing, just a different way of saying it. For the crime of striking me and calling me worthless, before I completely obliterate you, I will be taking away your ability to communicate. I will then chain you to that post behind me and watch as people try to communicate with you as they try in vain to extricate you from your situation."

He grabbed her, threw her over his shoulder and walked the short distance to the post sticking out of the ground behind him. Throwing her against the pole he laughed as she grunted in pain and picked up some chains off the ground. Wrapping them around her tightly, he locked it with a large padlock before walking over to a tree and pulling out an acetylene torch and its accoutrements and dragged them back to the post.

He looked up her and signed, "You understand why I am doing this to you?" She shook her head and he sighed loudly. He bent over and busied himself with the welding tools before straightening up and looking her square in the face. With one hand he signed once more, "Do you understand why I am doing this to you?" She shook her head again violently. He reached into his pocket and pulled out a flint striker and lit the torch. She stared in horror as he brought it to the chains and proceeded to melt the lock just enough to prevent a key from being used. He then welded the key onto the top of the padlock before turning it off and setting it on the ground.

Straightening up he looked around and signed, "Well, I should get this done with so I can go watch from a distance. He tossed a puzzle piece onto the ground and once again reached into his pocket. Pulling out a pair of garden shears he had stolen from Mike's little garden shed, he walked up to her, grabbed her left hand, and started cutting off each of her fingers. She tried to scream but could not and started crying and thrashing frantically as he reached for her other hand and repeated the process. Dropping the shears he gathered up all of her fingers and bound them together with a piece of string before shoving them into her mouth making her look as if she had an oddly shaped protruding tongue.

He stood back to admire his handiwork and reached out to slap her to stop her from trying to push them out of her mouth. He took up the welding torch again and passed the flame over her bleeding stumps causing her to buck under the agony before he yanked the fingers out of her mouth and burned the severed ends.

He signed, "This is in case someone kills me before you die and they try to reattach your fingers. One way or another, you are never regaining the use of them."

He then shoved the burned finger back into her mouth and wrapped a piece of clear tape around her head and across her mouth to prevent her from spitting them out. Stepping back to admire his handiwork he dropped his tools onto the ground and turned walking away into the nearest building to look out the window and watch.

Within ten minutes the remaining counselor and two campers were trying to get her down as she cried. Every time they had tried to remove the tape from her head he shot a bullet into the ground at their feet from his hiding place. Finally they gave up and started to run; as they ran he stepped out of the building and yelled after them. They turned in their headlong flight to safety and saw who the killer was and doubled their speed. He pointed the gun at them and shot them each in the back watching as they fell. Approaching them he reached down and snapped each of their necks then sorted out their particular pieces of the puzzle and dropped them on the ground next to their lifeless bodies.

Turning he looked at Marcy. Walking back to her he dropped the now empty gun onto the ground and stopped in front of her. Laughing up into her sobbing face he held up the torch once more and held it to her clothes, lighting her on fire. As she became a raging inferno he turned and reached for his knife and made a few shallow slashes on the top of his lower arms, threw the knife into Marcy's burning corpse and squeezed the cuts to make them bleed more profusely. He ripped his shirt off and ran inside the small cabin leaving a short trail of blood. He then tore his shirt into ribbons and used them to bind his arms up, crawled under the bed and started crying with fake terror.

Thirteen campers left to die. All counselors and various employees were now dead.

SEVENTEEN

The killer watched as Freddy ran from him, hobbled as he was from the ropes that were only partially tied around his ankles and his wrists. He had managed to catch him by surprise and caught the killer in the face with a glancing blow from his elbow before running off. Getting up off the ground he slowly walked after him knowing he couldn't get too far before he caught up to him. When he was in the fifth grade Freddy's girlfriend Angela had told him that he was hitting on her, which was absurd.

Freddy had come into the classroom where he was at waiting for class to begin and punched him in the face and most of the students had laughed. Unfortunately the teacher had not been in the room at the time and could not have prevented it. Those kids who had laughed at him were already dead or would be killed shortly. His next victim would be Angela. He had her tied up on the ground back where he had picked himself up off the ground.

Freddy fell to the ground finally and the killer ran the last few steps to him plunging a knife into his lower back effectively paralyzing him. He yanked the knife out of his back, rolled him over onto his back and slit his throat with no further thought.

Turning, he walked back to where Angela lay on her side crying and screaming for Freddy. She started struggling harder as she watched her death looming before her. Straddling her he stared down at her and sneered.

"You stupid bitch caused me to suffer constant humiliation and torture for most of my school career because you thought I was hitting on you. All I wanted from you was friendship you filthy cow. I am GAY!" He lashed out and punched her in the face as Freddy had done all those years ago, over and over again. When she finally lost consciousness he threw up on her.

When he had finally heaved out his guts

he stared down at her in disgust. He reached down and started scooping his vomit off of her and shoveling it into her mouth until she started choking. After he got it all in there he covered her mouth and nose with one hand and held her head back with the other until she vomited and promptly started to choke. Finally she aspirated and he watched her die in agony as her lungs slowly filled with fluid. With one final act of hatred he plunged the knife down into her throat and ripped it wide open, pulling the knife out and wiping it on her shirt. He then dropped her puzzle piece on top of her and slowly walked back over to Freddy and threw a puzzle piece on him as well.

EIGHTEEN

The killer looked up at the sky and realized daylight was fast approaching. He needed to speed this along and he still had eleven people left to kill. Sheila was to be his next victim and he saw her just ahead of him hiding out under a wheelbarrow. She had failed three times and was now a twenty year old senior, but what she had done to him was much worse. She had been his babysitter a few times and one night she decided to crawl naked into bed with him and start playing with him. Then in order to keep him from talking she had scared him half to death on multiple occasions by showing him horror movies and telling him the various things that happened in those movies would be done to him and even showed him the tools she would use on him; for instance a hand saw which she brought out to threaten him with repeatedly.

As he slowly approached her hiding place

he gripped a rock in his right hand and grabbed the edge of the wheelbarrow and flung it off of her suddenly. In a move just as quickly he struck her on the temple, not hard enough to kill her, but it was enough to stun her momentarily.

Dragging her limp body over to the sawhorses against the side of a small workshop they had built there, he dropped her on the ground. He walked into the workshop and grabbed a sturdy good sized board and a handsaw. When he went back outside he saw her body was gone. He dropped the items he was carrying and looked around for her and saw her brother Travis was trying to run off with her. He pulled out his knife, took careful aim, then flung it lodging it into the back of his thigh. Racing over to Travis and Sheila as they crumbled to the ground, he struck Travis on the head knocking him out.

Dragging their bodies back to the workshop one at a time was tedious and laborious; Travis was a pretty tall and very big guy. Finally he got them both where he needed them to be and turned away from them. Grabbing the board he placed it across the sawhorses. Deciding he needed to make it more stable he went back into the workshop and grabbed some nails and a hammer. Walking back outside he put the board up on the sawhorses and then nailed it down. He then grabbed Travis first and after a few minutes managed to get him up onto his makeshift table before he finally grabbed Sheila and positioned her on top of her brother with their eyes level with one another. Going back into the workshop he grabbed several lengths of rope and tied them down to the table in various locations.

Stepping back he waited until they both woke up, grabbed the hammer and nails and proceeded to nail their hands and feet to the table causing them both to scream. When he was satisfied they were going nowhere he got out his roll of tape, taped their eyes open and then wrapped it around their heads until they would not be able to stop looking into each other's eyes.

"Travis, for knowing full well what your sister had gotten up to during the years she babysat me, you shall die. Sheila for molesting me and constantly threatening to kill me, you shall also die. Travis, I was going to simply kill you out of hand, no fuss no muss, but you had to get involved. Now you get to watch as she dies, slowly and agonizingly and then experience the same fate as she does."

He grabbed the saw and started to saw through Sheila, their screams echoing around the island. Finally she was done and he continued cutting through to Travis and all the way through the board until they were both lying in halves apart from one another on the ground. Reaching into his pocket he pulled out the puzzle pieces, found theirs and tossed them onto their bodies before running off in search of his next victim.

NINETEEN

Taking a break he went into the Mess Hall and prepared a sandwich then sat and stared down at the puzzle while eating. He had known most of these people throughout his entire life, except one or two of the campers and most of the counselors. They all had to go though. Collateral damage was bound to happen when you took on an endeavor like this. He still needed to kill Jimmy, the middle child, brother to Travis and Sheila. He had already slit their parent's throats, Jim and Julie, the day before he left for camp. He had camped outside their house hiding in a tree for hours before the siblings finally left. Travis and Jimmy were already gone from high school, but they still came to camp as there was no age limit really, though most campers were under the age of eighteen.

As he stood up and brushed crumbs off of his shirt front, the door opened and who should walk in but Jimmy, just the person he was looking for. Jimmy stopped when he saw him and paused a moment then came all the way in and shut the door behind him. The killer had already changed clothes; in fact he had changed clothes multiple times through the night as he needed to be able to get close to his victims on several occasions and do it without raising suspicions.

Jimmy walked up to him looking scared and stared down at the puzzle. The killer reached out and removed the puzzle piece with Jimmy's face on it and replaced it with a blood splattered one. Jimmy continued to stare at the puzzle before slowly turning his head to stare down at the killer. Before he could react however, the killer slid the knife into his lower back, stepped back and yanked it out of him before starting to stab him over and over again. Finally Jimmy was a bloody corpse on the ground and the killer had to walk into the kitchen once again, go into the pantry and change clothes. As he left the Mess

Hall he couldn't help but reach out and kick Jimmy in the face, shattering several of his teeth in the process.

TWENTY

On the other side of the island was a small little abandoned church and this is where the killer headed to next knowing full well who he would find hiding in it. As luck would have it when he looked in through one of the broken windows he saw four of his victims inside; Jay, the other Kay, Barbara and Aiden. These four had constantly tortured him and harassed him for being an Atheist and were always constantly preaching at him. Along the walls were several large crosses hanging up and one planted squarely in the floor directly behind the tipped over podium. Sneaking inside he walked as slowly as possible to prevent the floor from creaking and snuck up behind the four kneeling in front of the cross. In quick succession he knocked each one of them out.

He searched around and finally had to build a makeshift ladder and dragged the body of

Mitch over to one cross on the side of the church. Lifting him up he tied him to the cross and proceeded to do the same to all of them, leaving Jay for the center cross behind the podium. After they were all tied to the crosses he woke them up quickly as he nailed their hands and feet to the crosses and stood back to admire his work.

Slipping back outside he grabbed the fishing spear he had brought with him from one of the yachts and walked back inside. Walking around the church he drove it deep into their sides before stopping in front of Jay. Filled with an intensely white hot rage he started stabbing him all over the body with it until Jesse was finally a mutilated and bloody corpse pouring his blood out onto the floor. Kay, Mitch and Barbara were all screaming fearing he would do the same to them. Instead he left the church and grabbed a can of gasoline he had left outside the front door. He proceeded to pour it all over the pews and floor inside the church then doused as much of the outside of the building as he could then set it ablaze and wandered off in search of his next victims. Their puzzle pieces were already part of the puzzle back in the Mess Hall.

TWENTY ONE

The only four people left alive on the island, other than the killer himself of course, were Scott, Trent, John and Paul. Each of these people he had at one time or another dated. John was the first of the four, so he went off in search of him. Finally he found him asleep in his bunk in his small cabin. Walking over to the sleeping figure he sat on the edge of the bed next to him watching his chest go up and down in an easy rhythm. He gently reached out and shook him awake.

John's eyelids fluttered open and it took him a minute to focus, but when he finally did he said, "David is that you?"

The killer, David, nodded and said, "Yes, it is me. I have a question for you."

John sat up slowly and smiled at him. His heart raced a thousand miles an hour as it always had when he looked at John.

"Do you think you and I could ever be a couple again? We were always good together you know?" David met John's eyes for a moment then dropped them to his lap at the sadness he saw there.

"David, I can't be gay, at least not openly, ever. My family would never understand. I am sorry, but you do know how much I love you, right?"

David looked up at him again and held out his hand with a sad smile on his face. John looked down at his hand then held his open as David dropped a bloody puzzle piece into his hand. He looked down at it, then back up at David and started to cry. David quickly placed his hands around John's throat and strangled him. When he was sure John was dead, he snapped his neck to be sure of it, then curled up with him to cry out his hurt.

TWENTY TWO

Scott was an easy kill. He simply found him curled up under some laundry in the laundry facility and rammed a pair of scissors into the bitchy little queens brain through his eye socket. At this point he had completed the puzzle in the Mess Hall as no one else would likely be in there and only Paul and Trent were left.

He found Paul down at the beach sitting there quietly staring out at the ocean.

Before he could approach him Paul said, "I knew it had to be you. Every person killed was either someone you didn't know so the deaths were random or they were people who have seriously hurt you and you did something to them in particular something that had happened to you in a roundabout way by their hands.

"When we had sex and I didn't tell you I was HIV positive, even after you confronted me when you found out, I ran and ran until I could not run any longer. After my parents brought me back here I figured something would eventually happen to me but I had no idea I would get sicker." Paul turned and faced David. I know you never got sick from me, but I was still sick and in fact since I never bothered taking care of myself I got even sicker. I have less than a month to live really and if you look closely you will be able to tell the signs."

David had already seen the signs of impending death on Paul so it was not news to him. "Paul, I could care less that you are HIV positive. The reason I am going to kill you now is because you deserve to die a quick and painless death at something other than some fatal disease. I am killing you also because instead of staying and working things out with me, because we would have been good together. You were scared and ran, leaving me behind. I could have taken care of you. However, you chickened out like a coward."

Paul looked stunned a bit, but nodded and

said, "I guess that I could have done, but I was scared." He lowered his head then stood up and stared David right in the eyes. "Do what you need to do. I would rather this any given day than slowly wasting away an agonizing death."

David stepped forward and shoved his knife into Paul's chest then caught him as he slid to the ground and held him until the last breath finally slipped from him. Kissing him on the forehead he strained to listen to Paul as he breathed out one last thing. "Thank you."

"You are welcome Paul. Maybe in the next life you will have the strength and courage to never run from your problems. Hell, maybe you can go on a murderous rampage like me." Paul probably only heard the first sentence because after he said his name he felt the body go limp. Laying him gently on the beach sand he stood up and brushed the sand from his pants then hands. Looking down at Paul he shed a single tear, wiped it away aggressively and went in search of Trent.

TWENTY THREE

He caught up to Trent as he was coming out of the Mess Hall. Trent stared at him in disgust, but obviously decided there was safety in numbers.

"The killer turned out to be Scott," he told Trent.

Trent looked shocked but then said, "It figures that bitchy little queen would snap and kill people one day. Where is he?"

David looked him square in the eye and said, "I killed him when he tried to kill me. I found a boat over next to the main dock. It is a small motorboat, but it should get us somewhere within range to get help. Let's get out of here." Trent nodded and together they raced off to the main dock.

David got into the boat and reached under a small tarp and felt the item he had placed there earlier; it was still there. Nodding slightly with grim satisfaction he watched as Trent got into the boat and then David started up the motor and they pulled away from the dock.

After a half an hour the engine died and they started drifting gently as the sun came up slowly. Trent yawned and said, "Should we try the radio again?"

Nodding David pulled the radio out and checked it. After five minutes a voice squawked back at them and David said, "In need of rescue." He then rattled off enough information to give them some idea as to where they were. As Trent turned to look out over the bow of the boat David reached under the tarp and pulled out a clothing iron.

"You remember when I broke up with you a few months ago and you tackled me on our friend's bed and tried to bash my skull in with an iron?" Trent turned slowly in the boat and saw the iron in his hand. "Well, let us just say Scott couldn't kill a fucking fly without injuring himself" Lashing out with the iron he took Trent by surprise and smashed him in the face. Blood spurted out and he then took the iron and wrapped the cord around his neck and strangled him. When he stopped breathing he tied off the cord and pushed him overboard. He slipped into the water himself to rinse himself off of blood and climbed back aboard.

Five minutes later a Coast Guard vessel showed up and picked him up. As he was questioned about the events of the night, he was taken back to the mainland and other vessels were sent off to investigate the island. Giving them an hour he finally pulled his cell phone out and placed a phone call. After the third ring on each call he would hang up and place another call. Each call triggered a bomb destroying the island piece by piece along with the members of the investigative squad that were there. When frantic reports started coming in he slipped out in the ensuing chaos.

EPILOGUE

Ten Years Later

"So, your name is Louis? Mine is Mark. Nice to meet you Louis." Mark held his hand out for Louis to shake.

After shaking his hand he said, "So Mark, I have a sailing yacht down in the harbor. Would you care to go sailing with me?"

Smiling Mark said, "I would love to! Where did you learn?"

"Oh, when I was a teenager in New York I went to summer camp with a bunch of my old schoolmates. You could say sailing is in my blood forever. It is a puzzle to me." He grinned at the confused look on Mark's face and said, "How about this weekend? We can sail out just far enough and watch the surfer boys surfing on the North Shore beaches. Have you ever been out of Honolulu?"

Mark nodded his head and said, "Yes

actually. I used to live at a campground with my mother until someone tried to drown me in the lake. I took care of the grounds for my mother. I had to clear out intruders all the time and clean up a lot of messes left behind. It got so I was good at using a machete. I go back once a year and make sure no one disturbs the place, and when they do I get rid of them."

Louis nodded and said, "I do the same thing on the island I learned to sail at."

Holding out his hand he said, "David. Nice to meet you."

Studying the hand held out Mark finally took it and said grinning, "Jason."

Yes, this story is disturbing, graphic and dark. It was done this way on purpose. I needed to vent my hurt and anger out on certain people in my past before I could begin to heal and I figured it was more constructive to destroy them on paper than by doing it in person. Thank you for listening. - David

www.ingramcontent.com/pod-product-compliance
Lightning Source LLC
Chambersburg PA
CBHW070522130626
46555CB00003B/1303